W0038593

ISBN-10: 1530306078
ISBN-13: 978-1530306077

DISCLAIMERS

- Absolutely nothing in this volume is meant to constitute legal, financial, or medical advice nor are the opinions presented to be considered expert opinions.

- This volume is **NOT** meant to be a replacement for the upcoming book, we believe our readers guide and critical analysis will increase interest in the upcoming book and not detract from it.

- In this volume, each particular detail is presented to the best of our knowledge and understanding of the upcoming book in the Potter series. If you think any of our analysis, or review is inaccurate **please email us** and we will correct it and publish an updated edition after we verify (slimreads@gmail.com).

- <u>Most importantly</u>: absolutely no portion of this summation volume was written in a Starbucks.

CONTENTS

INTRO: The Upcoming Play

Harry Potter is back! The entire Potter Mania world rejoiced when news came out that British author, J.K. Rowling, is all set to surprise them with another incredible story. The revelation that a stage play based on Harry Potter is underway was earlier made in December, 2013. The upcoming stage play was officially confirmed on the 18th anniversary of the UK publication of the first "Harry Potter" book, 26 June 2015.

The play titled *"Harry Potter and the Cursed Child"* is the eighth part of the Harry Potter series and scripted by the J.K Rowling in collaboration with John Tiffany, who will direct the production and Jack Thorne, who has written the resulting play. It will be staged in two parts- I and II. Part I and II are intended to be seen in order on the same day (matinee and evening) or on two consecutive evenings.

The Potter fans, desperately waiting for another story (I being one of them), went crazy with delight when confirmation came that it is the official sequel to Harry Potter and the Deathly Hallows as the eighth story of the series on October 23, 2015. It would receive its official world premiere on **Saturday, 30 July 2016** at Palace Theatre, Shaftesbury Avenue London (*Image Right*), on the 20th anniversary of the UK publication of Harry Potter and the Philosopher's Stone. The show's premiere production is scheduled to begin previews on 7 June 2016.

CHAPTER 1: The Announcement

This is the very first Harry Potter story that will be presented on a theatrical stage. This is also the first Harry Potter tale **not** written **solely by JK Rowling**. In the official announcement of the play, J.K. Rowling confirmed that new play called Harry Potter and the Cursed Child will be opening in London and due to its epic nature, it will be in two parts!

Rowling revealed that the play would explore the previously untold story of Harry's early years as an orphan and outcast. She is confident that when audiences see Harry Potter and the Cursed Child, they will understand why we this story has been told in this way. Director John Tiffany justified that the play will be presented in two parts as it shares a scale and ambition with all the Harry Potter stories.

Commenting on the project, Thorne, Rowling and Tiffany (*Image-Left*) said in a press release: "It is very exciting to explore Harry's world in a brand new way through the live form of theatre. Collaborating on this story is exhilarating for all of us and we can't wait to present the eighth story at the Palace Theatre."

CHAPTER 2: The Eighth Book

For J.K. Rowling's devoted readers, the next highlight is that the eighth Harry Potter book is going to be released nine years after JK Rowling's final story, The Deathly Hallows. Yeah, that right!! J.K. Rowling has just announced that she will be publishing the script of the upcoming stage play Harry Potter and the Cursed Child. Rowling's website **Pottermore** confirmed this script will be the eighth book in the series. The hardback edition of **"Harry Potter and the Cursed Child - Parts I & II"** will be released on July 31 after the stage play has debuted the day before in London's West End.

Releasing simultaneously with the opening of the play, the book will give Potter fans chance to indulge once again in the adventures of their favourite wizard without having to be in London. The publication will also bring joy to those fans in the UK, who were not able to get tickets to the Live Play. Little, Brown UK is publishing the book, and according to Guardian, it has already **hit No. 1 on book charts** a day after the announcement.

There were speculations that Harry Potter and the Cursed Child is a prequel. Rowling however clarified, the confusion surrounding the latest book after the news broke out that it is not a prequel, and it is definitely not a novel:

> **To be clear! The SCRIPT of #CursedChild is being published. #NotANovel #NotAPrequel ????** https://t.co/3OhdOBIqJt - *J.K. Rowling (@jk_rowling) February 11, 2016.*

Print and digital editions published will comprise of the version of the play script at the time of the play's preview performances. The e-book edition will be published by the famous Harry Potter fan site *Pottermore*.

CHAPTER 3: The Harry Potter Era Begins Again

The Era of Harry Potter has not ended after all...!!! The declaration by JK Rowling that the seventh and the last book "Harry Potter and the Deathly Hallows" brings about inevitable ending to Harry Potter series had shattered the hearts of millions of die-hard Potter fans.

But now that J.K. Rowling is writing a play as a sequel to the Seven-part series, the mania is back again. Rowling announced that the script of the play will in fact, be released as a two-part book on **July 31, 2016**. The play is  set 19 years after the end of Harry Potter and the Deathly Hallows, the series' final book.

The Harry Potter and the Deathly Hallows narrates how Harry, Ron and Hermione after abandoning Hogwarts, embark on their journey to hunt and destroy Voldemort's four remaining Horcruxes. They come across the three mythical objects, collectively known as the "Deathly Hallows" – The Elder Wand, the Resurrection Stone and the Invisibility Cloak. The end concludes with final confrontation between Harry, master of the Elder Wand and Voldemort, Voldemort is put to death forever with the rebound of his own final Killing Curse.

In the epilogue to Deathly Hallows, Harry and married Ginny Weasley are seen married and together they had two sons, James and Albus, and a daughter, Lily. Ron and Hermione also have two children, Rose and Hugo. Harry's younger son Albus is starting his first year at Hogwarts, and is worried about the Sorting into the houses. The "Boy who lived" is a hero and a symbol of hope for the magical world even 19 years after the downfall of "He Who must Not Be Named". Like a classic fairy-tale, the book ends in a good note with the words: **"The scar had not pained Harry for nineteen years. All was well."**

There has been a lot **speculation and expectation** from the plot of this new story. The Cursed Child will pick up from that moment, focusing on Harry as an overworked Ministry of Magic employee- Auror and his younger son Albus Severus, who is struggling under the pressure of the family legacy. The play will explore how Harry wrestles with his past.

The claim by Rowling that it is a new story and not a rehash of the previous content has taken a suspense toll. Fans are excited to know about the lives of Harry, Ron and Hermione as adults and parents. The stress on the story is pointing towards Harry's **relationship with his son Albus** as they struggle to come to terms with Potter's past. There are even rumours about a rift between his two sons, since Albus is more like his father, and James being the elder one, is expected to be mirror image of the famous Harry Potter. So it is only natural that fans expect Albus to take the story of our favourite wizard forward.

Whatever be the plot, fans are just as excited to read the play script as they would be for a new fiction novel. The on-stage play unfolding the fantasy and magical world of Harry Potter live, will be worth the wait. The Cursed Child is still a continuation of The Harry Potter story, and Potter world are really inquisitive to see how Rowling's dialogue for the stage will work on the page.

CHAPTER 4: Who is the Cursed Child?

The question Potter world has been clamouring on is "who is this cursed child".

But J.K. Rowling didn't get where she was by giving up secrets so readily. Fans out there still have no idea who he is. (Or she? That could conceivably be a girl.)

When the first **official Artwork** (*Image above*) of the Harry Potter and the Cursed Child artwork was unveiled, an interesting detail was the Golden Snitch-like design. Minds flew to the Resurrection Stone hidden in a Golden Snitch in Harry Potter and the Deathly Hallows. Maybe this kid has something to do with that Snitch, if he managed to find it? Or is it just a reference to Quidditch?

Rowling has previously hinted that the Cursed Child is someone we're familiar with, but ruled out Voldemort as the titular character. The official synopsis gave a clearer picture that strongly suggests Harry's son Albus is the Cursed Child, which in retrospect makes perfect sense. Now fans can move on to more important questions like: Is Albus Potter the "Cursed Child" and who will play him on stage?

CHAPTER 5: Play Synopsis

The official synopsis released on 23 October 2015 is as follows:

It was always difficult being Harry Potter and it isn't much easier now that he is an overworked employee of the Ministry of Magic, a husband, and father of three school-age children.

While Harry grapples with a past that refuses to stay where it belongs, his youngest son Albus must struggle with the weight of a family legacy he never wanted. As past and present fuse ominously, both father and son learn the uncomfortable truth: sometimes, darkness comes from unexpected places.

What last HP book left us with was Harry waving off his sons, James Sirius and Albus Severus, at Platform Nine and Three-Quarters, Kings Cross Station, The upcoming stage play holds a lot of surprises in store. The stage is set for an adult, middle aged Harry with three children, Harry is 36 year old, overworked Ministry of Magic employee.

Speculation that the play might centre on Harry's early life with the Dursleys has been cleared up by the news that the story actually centres on his middle son Albus Severus *(Image left)*. It looks like Albus, will face peculiar difficulties because of his father's past. Based on that short synopsis alone, it is possible that Albus may have to deal with the fact that his father Harry till 18 years of age was a Horcrux.

Fans are obviously expecting trouble for all the children

as they enter into the new term at Hogwarts, so this "curse" could also stem from something else entirely. Also, Jack Thorne — who is writing the play together with Rowling — is a fantastic playwright who loves to explore themes of loneliness and isolation. Fans can expect Albus to be a melancholy, burdened child who just has too much to live up to.

There is also a mention of Harry's live before he joins the Wizardry World. Enough curiosity has been built up about his past as an orphan.

The story possibly will also narrate the lives of Harry's murdered parents. It will delve into what happened to Harry's parents — Lily Evans Potter and James Potter — before they were killed by Lord Voldemort, forcing an infant Harry to be raised in miserable circumstances by his mother's sister, Petunia, her horrid husband Vernon and their spoiled son Dudley.

The complicated relationship between siblings Lily and Petunia may be talked about in detail. It is clearly evident throughout the course of the seven Harry Potter books that a Muggle like the rest of her family, Petunia was always put out by her sister's magical powers.

There is also dramatic fodder in the friendship between Lily and Severus Snape during their schooldays at Hogwarts. The Deathly Hallows gave a preview of how Snape helped Lily refine her magical powers. It became clear he carried a torch for her. But though she cared for him, she did not love him. Instead, she fell for James Potter, who she once disliked for his cockiness.

Another of their friends, Remus Lupin may have a space of his own in the story. The roles are perfect for up-and-coming young actors. Lily was just 20 when Harry was born, and a year older when she and husband James were slain.

In addition, in a 2014 piece on the Pottermore site, Rowling sketched out what might have become of the main characters too: Harry now **an Auror** – a member of an elite unit of specialist officers trained to apprehend Dark Wizards - and reluctantly enjoying with Ron (**who runs a joke shop**) and Hermione (**now deputy head of the Department of Magical Law Enforcement**) the status of gradually greying celebs. So the Potter mania World is bound to imagine the upcoming story on those lines. So the saga continues!

CHAPTER 6: Production, Casting and the Creative Team

The **cast of the play** has been the most hyped-about aspect of "Harry Potter and the Cursed Child". Potter Mania world has been really eager to know who will be replacing their  favourite starts as their adult counterparts in the theatrical event. Surprisingly this has been a source of controversy.

The principal characters will be played by theatre actor **Jamie Parker** as Harry, Olivier Award-winning actress **Noma Dumezweni** as Hermione, English, and film and TV actor **Paul Thornley** as Ron.

| Jamie Parker | Noma Dumezweni | Paul Thornley |

The Tiffany team struck a blow for diversity by casting the Swaziland-born Dumezweni as Hermione. Hermione

Granger as a black has been given mixed reactions by fans, whereas some are critical, some fans think it's not a big deal while some also welcome the change. The casting of a **black actress as Hermione** was not entirely unexpected for some fans though. There are blogs such as Black Girl Dangerous, which suggest that women of colour identify with Hermione.

When the casting was announced, JK Rowling responded to fans' questions of how she felt about "black Hermione" with this tweet: "Canon: brown eyes, frizzy hair and very clever. White skin was never specified. Rowling loves black Hermione." She pointed out that the character's race was never actually specified in the books. Emma Watson, who played the character in the films, has praised the casting choice, writing on Twitter - "Can't wait to see Noma Dumezweni as Hermione on stage this year. Though at first, the decision to cast Black Hermione was taken in criticism, but now it is being gladly accepted by Potter World.

The role of redhead Ron has being essayed strawberry blonde; Paul Thornley has also raised many eyebrows. The red hair of Ron, which is prominent in all Harry books, has been totally overlooked in the casting of the play. Only time will tell, how suitable this casting is.

Parker currently stars in the West End show Guys and Dolls, and his film credits include Valkyrie, The History Boys (which he also starred in onstage), and Le Weekend. Dumezweni is leading the Royal Court Theatre's Linda. She appeared in Dirty Pretty Things, and has guest-starred on Casualty, Doctor Who, and EastEnders. Thornley stars in London Road, after originating the same role onstage, and is now shooting The Crown for Netflix.

The play is being produced by **Sonia Friedman**, a British West End and Broadway theatre produce, and **Collin Callender**, an English television, film, and theatre producer working primarily in the United States.

Production & Creative Team

Sonia Friedman
Producer

Christine Jones
Set Design

Collin Callender
Producer

Neil Austin
Lighting

Steven Hoggett
Coreographer

Gareth Fry
Sound Design

Katrina Lindsay
Costume Designer

Jeremy Chernick
Special Effects

Along with over cast that is over 30, the crew has plenty of experienced talent involved. Steve Hoggett (movement) has worked on *The Twits*, *Let the Right One In* and *Black Watch* among others. Christine Jones (set design) has done *Let the Right One In* and *Spring Awakening* over here and *American Idiot* on Broadway. Katrina Lindsay (costumes) worked on stage adaptations of *Bend It Like Beckham* and *American Psycho*. She won praise from critics for her work on the new hit British musical "Bend It Like Beckham", which is on at the Phoenix. Rounding out the gang are Neil Austin (lighting), Gareth Fry (sound) and Jeremy Chernick (special effects).

CHAPTER 7: Future Business Prospects

The Harry Potter franchise is one of the world's biggest literary success stories, with more than 450 million hardcopies sold worldwide. The film versions were also record-breaking, making more than **$7.0 billion (6.3 billion Euros)** at the box office.

So it is very obvious, that a similar future prospect is expected out of "Harry Potter and the Cursed Child". The play is regarded as the most entertaining and awaited theatrical event of 2016. Its opening in July 2016 will attract a box-office advance the likes of which hasn't been seen in London before. Fans have booked tickets like crazy and those outside London are already pre-ordering the Print edition.

Release Date	Movie	Production Budget	Domestic Opening Weekend	Domestic Box Office	Worldwide Box Office	Trailer
Nov 16, 2001	Harry Potter and the Sorcerer's Stone	$125,000,000	$90,294,621	$317,575,550	$974,755,371	
Nov 15, 2002	Harry Potter and the Chamber of Secrets	$100,000,000	$88,357,488	$261,987,880	$878,979,634	
Jun 4, 2004	Harry Potter and the Prisoner of Azkaban	$130,000,000	$93,687,367	$249,538,952	$796,688,549	
Nov 18, 2005	Harry Potter and the Goblet of Fire	$150,000,000	$102,685,961	$290,013,036	$896,911,078	
Jul 11, 2007	Harry Potter and the Order of the Phoenix	$150,000,000	$77,108,414	$292,004,738	$942,943,935	
Jul 15, 2009	Harry Potter and the Half-Blood Prince	$250,000,000	$77,835,727	$301,959,197	$935,083,686	Play
Nov 19, 2010	Harry Potter and the Deathly Hallows: Part I	$125,000,000	$125,017,372	$295,001,070	$959,301,070	Play
Jul 15, 2011	Harry Potter and the Deathly Hallows: Part II	$125,000,000	$169,189,427	$381,011,219	$1,341,511,219	Play
Nov 18, 2016	Fantastic Beasts and Where to Find Them			$0	$0	
Nov 16, 2018	Fantastic Beasts and Where to Find Them 2			$0	$0	
	Totals	$1,155,000,000		$2,389,091,642	$7,726,174,542	
	Averages	$144,375,000	$103,022,047	$298,636,455	$965,771,818	

The box office Statistics –Taken from the-numbers.com

It has already proved to be a success with an initial round of **175,000 tickets sold in October, 2015 within 24 hours of** booking opening. Producers released a second batch, available to fans who had registered for priority booking. A third set is still to go on sale but the date is yet to be announced.

The script from the Harry Potter play has leapt to the

top of bestseller lists, a day after its July release was announced. Just after the announcement was made, pre-orders have propelled it to **Number One** on the Amazon and Waterstones book charts. Infact the hard-back edition's pre-orders were expected to break all records.

    Harry Potter and the Cursed Child is coming as two plays that are opening in London. So when is "Harry Potter and the Cursed Child" going to Broadway? Of course it's going to the United States but when, is yet to be decided. It will be very successful since Harry Potter is beloved all over the world. Also both of the producing teams behind the project have done several successful West End-to-Broadway transitions before, too, so the future of this production is clearly not an afterthought.

CHAPTER 8: Tickets Details

The play managed to set a **West End record** when it sold 175,000 tickets in 24 hours. The tickets are just disappearing in a puff of smoke. The high demand for tickets prompted organizers to release tickets for performances between October 2016 and January 2017 to those registered for priority booking. It's now booking all the way up to **May 2017**. Great seats will be available from 21st September 2016 to 8th January 2017 and from 19th March 2017 to 18th May 2017.

The schedule of the plays is: On Wednesdays, Saturdays and Sundays there will be a matinee performance of Part I and an evening performance of Part II. One ticket will automatically secure the same seat for **Part I and II** on the same day. On Thursdays there will be an evening performance of Part I and on Fridays an evening performance of Part II. If you choose to see Part One on a Thursday evening, we will automatically book you into Part Two the following Friday evening. Tickets are priced from £10 all the way up to £130.

CHAPTER 9: Critical Interpretation

Rowling's Harry Potter series has ushered in its fair share of interpretations, controversy and backlash, most notable among them was the controversy it created in the Islamic and Christian community for its glorification of witchcraft. This backlash has helped to make Harry Potter the most banned book series in the world, giving Christians and Muslims something they can agree on.

Rather than a simple adventure story, these groups contend that Harry Potter makes witchcraft appealing, that the reading of these books (and viewing of their cinematic adaptations) may threaten the moral fabric of a suggestible youth.

These criticisms tend to ring hollow, however, as witchcraft plays a major role in much less controversial works of literature. For example, witchcraft is the major inciting incident in Macbeth and populates the golden brick road in The Wizard of Oz. Neither of these literary titles illicit any sort of backlash in the community.

The appeal of the bespectacled wizard may have little to do with witchcraft in and of itself, and more to do with **power**; the desire of the disenfranchised to feel powerful in powerless situations. Children typically feel powerless, always being told what to do, where to go, what to say and how to speak. The young pupils of Hogwarts have supernatural abilities that make them useful, able to compete on the adult stage. This same phenomenon may explain the popularity of superhero movies and the Star Wars franchise.

Child Abuse/Institutionalization Interpretation

There is another interpretation of the Harry Potter series that seems to illuminate and hold even more water. Two years ago "Mr_Broomstick" posted this fan theory, which has since gone viral, sparking both accolades and fierce debate. His article conluded:

I believe the Harry Potter series was written about the kind of experiences that institutionalized children encounter... Most people simply see it as an adventure story about magic. It's not about magic. It's about mental trauma and the delusion that results from it.

That is a pretty bold assertion but he does back it up pretty logically. He explains:

My theory is that this story line is a coded explication of a delusional boy that is starting to engage in violent outbursts, and is sent to a mental institution as a result. Everything that happens after that becomes increasingly detached from reality, and what we see, as the audience, is his delusion, which is a re-casting of his institutionalization experience into a kind of adventure.

I believe there is a great deal of evidence in the text for this hypothesis. Mental illness is featured just about everywhere in the series, and the theme of insanity is very prominent. Classic features of mental illness, such as delusions, paranoia and multiple-personality disorders become increasingly more important to the story line.

Then he goes on to provide a list of examples wherein these features of mental illness appear throughout the storyline:

♣ *The school is locked. It is also filled with random, insane dangers that everyone accepts as perfectly normal -- moving stairs,*

22

talking paintings, deadly monsters roaming around outside. Mental prisons are dangerous places where crazy situations are, in fact, ordinary.

♣ *Sirius Black is Harry's godfather, and is overtly insane.*

♣ *In the 4th book, Black is closely affiliated with (and introduced by and treated as a kind of surrogate for) a werewolf, who is obsessed with the moon. The moon is a symbol for insanity (i.e., lunacy).*

♣ *The Goblet of Fire contest pits students against each other in contests that are openly life-threatening, which is what students at a school for violent, mentally-disturbed children experience on a regular basis.*

♣ *The clean-cut Derek Diggery (a fantasy image of the popular, successful boy Harry could have been were it not for his mental problems) is murdered by "Voldemort," who is Harry's alter ego and the projection of his rage and fury. Harry is the only one who sees this event, and no one believes it was "Voldemort." This event is a metaphor for Harry murdering a boy who is too perfect, despised for having the life of love and ease that Harry wanted, but never got. So, he imagines that "Voldemort" did it. When no one believes him, it's an unspoken metaphor for the fact that everyone knows Harry is the murderer.*

♣ *If the murder of Derk Diggery is not meant to be a real event, but entirely imaginary in Harry's mind, then the murder of the normal boy is a metaphor for Harry losing his final chance at a normal life.*

♣ *This "murder" takes place in a maze where the main danger is being psychologically possessed and going insane.*

♣ Harry is helped in this unwanted fight to the death by "Mad Eye" Moody, who is also openly insane. To compound the insanity of this parent-surrogate, Moody is not actually the real Moody, but an imposter, who is even more openly insane.

♣ Book Five opens with Harry again attacking his brother/cousin Dudley, leaving him traumatized. Periodically, Harry returns to civilian life, but finds that he can't go five minutes without a seriously violent, delusional episode.

♣ This incident was interpreted by Harry as an attack by "Dementors" who cannot be seen by normal people. This incident causes Harry to appear before a board of inquiry to determine if he is too violent for Hogwarts, the alternative being Azkaban (i.e., a more harsh mental prison).

♣ Azkaban is heavily associated with insanity. In the story, it is said that inmates go crazy within days of arriving, which is a metaphor for saying that it is a high-security prison for violent mental patients. It is where Black and Lestrange (and others) went off the rails.

♣ It is also in the fifth book and movie that we meet Black's cousin Beatrix LeStrange, who is also openly insane. She murders the insane Sirius Black just as he is becoming more stable and normal. This is a metaphor for the violently delusional side of Harry's mind defeating and suppressing the side that might have healed.

♣ Harry's newest friend at school is Luna Lovegood, whose name is another reference to lunacy, and is openly known to be crazy, and is the only other student who can see Harry's delusions, even within the context of an otherwise crazy place like Hogwarts.

♣ Another "class" mate, Neville Longbottom, the forlorn loser, is *revealed to have a family history of mental illness -- parents who are mental patients, having been driven insane by Beatrix.*

♣ *Repeated references are made to "Voldemort" being so evil that he drives his victims crazy with torture, rather than merely killing them.*

♣ *It is repeatedly indicated that the boy "Tom Riddle" (the young "Voldemort") is actually Harry Potter, with constant parallels and similarities being heavily stressed. Same books, same wand, both orphaned, etc. Harry has increasing visions of Voldemort, and they even share thoughts, which is an obvious symbol for saying that "Voldemort" is just a component of Harry's diseased mind, at first only a whisper, and becoming increasingly dominant and thus real to him.*

♣ *In the 6th (or 7th?) book, I believe Rowling tried to tell us what she was really writing about -- there is a flashback scene where Dumbledore first meets "Voldemort," as a boy. Dumbledore comes to rescue the boy (who is really Riddle/Harry) from abuse and poverty. When Dumbledore says he has come to take him to a special school for kids with his kind of needs, Riddle's first response is that he knows Hogwarts is an insane anylum, and he doesn't want to go.*

And if all that weren't enough, consider this quote from the last book:

Harry says "Tell me one last thing. Was this real, or has this been happening inside my head?"

"Of course it is happening inside your head, Harry. But why on Earth should that mean it is not real."

If the Potter series is really about the institutionalization brought on by trauma-based childhood psychosis, and the delusions brought on by said institutionalization, exactly what sort of trauma could have caused such a psychotic adventure? The answer may be the key to finally understanding the Harry Potter series, and its ability to connect with so many readers. The post continues:

> *If we interpret the story as Harry's fantasy, then the Dursleys are Harry's real parents, and the Potters are imaginary. The Durselys either can't cope with the increasingly-delusional boy living with them, or perhaps they are merely abusive, and it's the abuse that's making him delusional. In any event, the parent-figures constantly mistreat him, favor the brother, and inflict endless cruelty and humiliation on him. One day, Harry snaps, and Dudley (who is really Harry's brother) is severely injured, in a way requiring repeated hospital treatments. (In the delusion, Harry imagines that a pig's tail is magically grown from Dudley's buttocks.) As a result of this incident, Harry is taken away to a 'special school.'*

> *At his new "school", Harry becomes obsessed with a mirror, where he spends endless days imagining his perfect parents. Of course, they are dead, which is a metaphor for saying they are wholly imaginary...*

Imaginary, or are they simply absent? Harry's real parents were killed by an evil wizard when Harry was just a baby, but just how relatable is that anyway? Parents are not usually prevented from raising their children by the spell of an evil wizard.

On the other hand, it *is* common (even typical) in today's world for children NOT to be raised by two loving-and-biological parents, but separated instead by voluntary absence, divorce, indifference, undetermined paternity and single-motherhood. This type of "orphan", as well as the ensuing trauma, is a lot more common (if somewhat less romantic).

Fatherless-Home Interpretation

A complementary interpretation is the **Fatherless-Home Interpretation** of the Potter series and has long gone unnoticed, and is it any wonder? <u>**Half of all marriages end in divorce**</u> saying nothing of the marriages that never were (in the case of **single-motherhood**). Broken and single-parent homes have become so prevalent in recent decades; like the forest for the trees, however, epidemics go unnoticed whenever they become the norm.

To say something is common, however, is not to say it is benign. These households are considerably more at risk than intact families to suffer from abuse and, in turn, to produce children that engage in abusive activity as adults. Here are just a few disturbing facts associated with fatherlessness:

- **82% of all rapists come from single-mother headed households** alone (of course, this is not to say that ALL children of single-parent households become rapists – but the inverse is nearly true, that nearly all rapists come from single-mother households). That leaves only 18% coming from divorced households, the foster system, and abusive two-parent households. I'm sure a few come from non-abusive intact families that act out of pure volition, but it seems that number is staggeringly small.

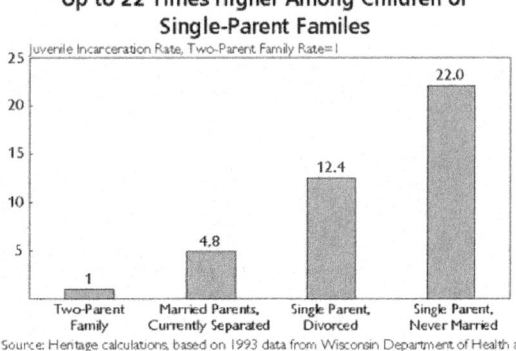

Chart 16

In Wisconsin, Juvenile Incarceration Rates Are Up to 22 Times Higher Among Children of Single-Parent Familes

Juvenile Incarceration Rate, Two-Parent Family Rate=1

Source: Heritage calculations, based on 1993 data from Wisconsin Department of Health and Human Services and U.S. Bureau of the Census, Current Population Survey.

- There is a correlation between **children of divorce and property crimes** *(which makes sense since no-fault divorce essentially is a property crime that, usually, the divorcing mother is committing against the children's father with the help of the government as it extracts alimony by force from the man she was "dissatisfied" with).*
- In a Wisconsin study, children of single-mothers were shown to be **22 times more likely** to be incarcerated (see chart above).
- In Britain, there was a study in the 1980s *(this type of data is getting harder to find lately because of the political-correctness shield surrounding single-mothers)* that indicated that a child, whose biological mother cohabits with a "partner" she is not married to, was **33 times more likely to suffer serious abuse** than a child with married parents (see chart below).

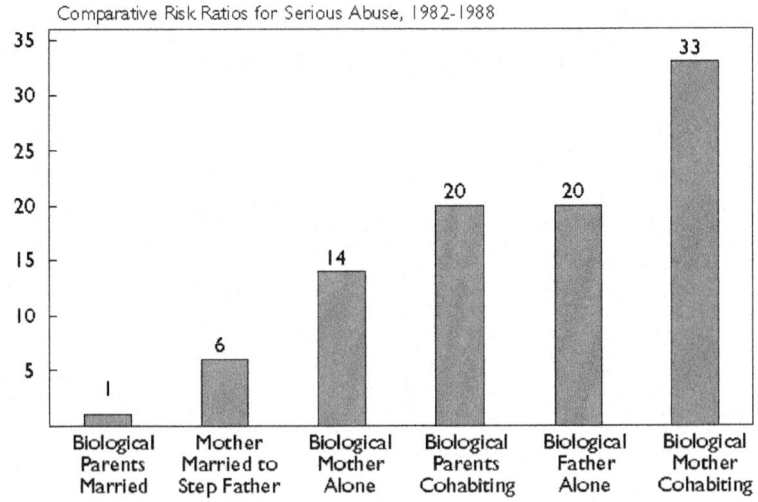

In Britain, a Child Whose Biological Mother Cohabits Was 33 Times More Likely to Suffer Serious Abuse Than a Child With Married Parents

Comparative Risk Ratios for Serious Abuse, 1982-1988

Family Structure

Source: Robert Whelan, *Broken Homes & Battered Children*, 1993.

The last chart about Britain (where Harry Potter is supposed to be from) really tells the story of how broken or fatherless homes are rife with painful and serious child abuse. What's more, it is a topic that most people shy away from which is shameful because child abuse is one of the most damaging of plagues on society. There is something called an Adverse Childhood Experience (ACE) test that produces an ACE number from 0 to 10 (the higher the number the more adverse childhood experiences the test taker has suffered). You can take the test at the following link:

http://www.theannainstitute.org/Finding%20Your%20ACE%20Score.pdf

If your score is higher than zero, than it doesn't mean you are doomed to live a life of crime and abusing others, not by a longshot. That said, it is important to not simply pretend that the adverse experience didn't occur. It is imperative to deal with childhood trauma; otherwise you are likely to continue the cycle of abuse, either by becoming an abuser or by self-erasing and enabling others to abuse you.

Just as children have been neglected by absentee parents, this problem has been neglected and ignored by society. More to the point, childhood trauma is marginalized in the story of Harry Potter.

The story of Harry Potter begins with a very bleak picture of his childhood abuse. Now the reality is that adoptive parents are not usually abusive and their children generally do almost as well as children from intact families since it tends to select people that really want to be parents (no one adopts by accident). On the other hand, abuse is **most common** among single-mothers who choose to cohabitate with an unmarried partner.

Therefore, in this interpretation, Harry's evil adoptive parents are really a **single-mother with a live-in boyfriend**. Any reference to his biological parents is a reference to the childhood he *could have had* if his single-mother and absent (and possibly unidentifiable) father had married before he was born and they stayed together (thus drastically reducing the chance of this type of traumatic childhood).

What is possibly even more disturbing than his depicted childhood of abuse is how the story acts as if this childhood has had no ill effects on our hero. Harry is locked in what is more-or-less a closet and his adoptive parents spew out scorn and vitriol without the slightest provocation.

And yet Harry is well-adjusted, polite, brave and sincere; in short, he demonstrates characteristics of a loved kid from a stable in-tact home. But where did those values come from? Where did he learn them?

Harry Potter and the Cursed Childhood

Harry Potter therefore becomes a fantasy of an entirely different sort, more fantastical than any magic spell, flying broom or invisibility cloak. Harry Potter is the fantasy of invisible trauma, the myth of unnecessary parents and well-adjusted orphans. When all is said and done, that fantasy is a lot harder to swallow.

This is not to say that volition does not play a part in human behavior. All too often people present the question of childhood development and resultant adult behavior as if the only possible factors are **Nature** and **Nurture**. This is often referred to as the **Nature-Nurture** debate.

However, this leaves out the most important factor (and the only factor you can really control) and that is **Volition** (the ability to choose for yourself).

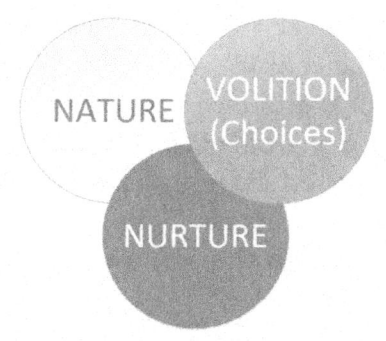

People have free will and choices to do good or bad are within all of us at all times regardless of genetics, background and upbringing.

Our focus on the effects of childhood trauma on the child's character and behaviour was not to diminish the role of volition, but to create awareness that ACEs are a dreadfully serious matter for those who have suffered through them.

This does not disable your ability to use volition to overcome your experience and create a better life for the next generation. On the contrary, if you are going to overcome something you must first be aware that the challenge exists. All too often people find it more comforting (and less disruptive to the neglecters and abusers surrounding them) to blame invisible forces rather than confront childhood trauma. We see this playing out before us as the country is stirring up claims of racism at a time when the KKK is lucky to find 3000 people in the entire country to join its ranks (and there are reports that indicate that a third to half of its members are comprised of federal infiltrators keeping tabs on the wacko group).

It is much more comforting to blame faceless "institutionalized" racism than to come to terms with one's own abusive or neglect-ridden childhood. For white people this manifests itself a little differently, usually in the form of blaming faceless "corporations" for all of their own failings. See, failing to launch has nothing to do with abuse, neglect, fatherlessness, or the choices you and those around you have been making; instead it is Walmart's fault.

While this line of thinking may be more comforting it is not more useful. Even if these claims of racism and corporatism have some basis in truth, they are certainly NOT the main reasons for your current lot. This becomes obvious, for example, when you normalize statistics by family arrangement. One example that comes to mind is black incarceration rates. While blacks are incarcerated at much higher levels than whites, when you compare just blacks raised by their **two Biological and Married Parents (BAMP)** with whites that were raised the same way, you find that blacks and whites are **incarcerated at pretty much the same rates**.

This illustrates that paternity, and not racism, is the main factor in the varying levels of incarceration between the races. Asians for example are hardly ever incarcerated compared to whites (not because cops hate whites but because Asians hardly ever divorce or have children out of wedlock).

What will be interesting to see in the new play is if the "Cursed Child" exhibits any of the traits of abused or neglected children when the curse is in effect. What will also be of interest is the family arrangement that is presented. In other words did this child enjoy an intact childhood? Did they have any Adverse Childhood Experiences? We can assume that Harry tried to be a good parent, but was he able to keep his own childhood trauma from spilling over into the next generation?

FREE GIFT SPECIAL REPORT

10 Little-Known Facts Even Potterheads Don't Know

Pop quiz hot shot! You think you know EVERYTHING about the Harry Potter series and its amazing rise in worldwide fandom? THINK AGAIN! I'm sure you know your Dumbledores from your Longbottoms but it is time to push your fandom to the next level (that's right, level 9 and 3/4)!

As our **free gift** for being a **SLIM READS enthusiast** we are happy to give you a special report about the **Little-Known Facts Even Potterheads Don't Know**.

Don't let Voldemort keep you from getting this awesome report!

Get your **free copy** at:

http://sixfigureteen.com/potter

<u>ALSO</u>: We will let you know about future Slim Reads titles so this is **win-win**! Enjoy your **FREE GIFT** and thank you for being part of the **SLIM READS** Family!

FREE GIFT SPECIAL REPORT
The Tidiest and Messiest Places on Earth

Parts of the Harry Potter series can get messy, but we made a special report about the Tidiest and Messiest Places on Earth! This report is a great supplement to that summary that is all about the virtues of being tidy.

As our **free gift** for being a **SLIM READS enthusiast** we are happy to give you a special report about the **3 Most Messy** and the **3 Most Tidy** places on Earth.

Learn about everything from **Garbage Island** to Computer-Chip **Clean Rooms** (and, of course, everything in between).

Get your **free copy** at:

http://sixfigureteen.com/messy

ALSO: We will let you know about future Slim Reads titles so this is **win-win**! Enjoy your **FREE GIFT** and thank you for being part of the **SLIM READS** Family!

CPSIA information can be obtained
at www.ICGtesting.com
Printed in the USA
LVOW13s1021141216
517222LV00022B/703/P